The First Strawberries

A · CHEROKEE · STORY

retold by **Joseph Bruchac**

pictures by **Anna Vojtech**

PUFFIN BOOKS

AUTHOR'S NOTE

Although I recall first hearing this story over a decade ago
(while talking with Mary and Goingback Chiltoskey,
Cherokee elders from North Carolina), the legend of the origin
of the first strawberries has been put down on paper
numerous times since it was first recorded in James Mooney's
Myths of the Cherokee (1900). More recently, Cherokee storytellers
Jean Starr, Gayle Ross, and Lloyd Arneach
helped me understand the story well enough to tell it.
—J.B.

PUFFIN BOOKS
Published by the Penguin Group
Penguin Putnam Inc., 375 Hudson Street, New York, New York 10014, U.S.A.
Penguin Books Ltd, 27 Wrights Lane, London W8 5TZ, England
Penguin Books Australia Ltd, Ringwood, Victoria, Australia
Penguin Books Canada Ltd, 10 Alcorn Avenue, Toronto, Ontario, Canada M4V 3B2
Penguin Books (N.Z.) Ltd, 182-190 Wairau Road, Auckland 10, New Zealand

Penguin Books Ltd, Registered Offices: Harmondsworth, Middlesex, England

First published in the United States of America by Dial Books for Young Readers,
a division of Penguin Books USA Inc., 1993
Published in Puffin Books, 1998

1   3   5   7   9   10   8   6   4   2

Text copyright © Joseph Bruchac, 1993
Illustrations copyright © Anna Vojtech, 1993
All rights reserved

THE LIBRARY OF CONGRESS HAS CATALOGED THE DIAL EDITION AS FOLLOWS:
Bruchac, Joseph
The first strawberries: a Cherokee story / retold by Joseph Bruchac ;
pictures by Anna Vojtech.—1st ed.   p.   cm.
Summary: A quarrel between the first man and the first woman is reconciled
when the Sun causes strawberries to grow out of the earth.
ISBN 0-8037-1331-2.—ISBN 0-8037-1332-0 (lib.)
1. Cherokee Indians—Legends. [1. Cherokee Indians—Legends. 2. Indians of North America—Legends.
3. Strawberries—Folklore.] I. Vojtech, Anna, ill. II. Title.
E99.C5B885 1993 398.2'089975—dc20 91-31058 CIP AC

Puffin Books ISBN 0-14-056409-8

Printed in the United States of America

The full-color artwork was prepared using watercolors and colored pencils.

*For my Tsalagi friends
and teachers—Wado!*
J.B.

To Roland
A.V.

LONG AGO when the world was new, the Creator made a man and a woman. The two of them were made at the same time so that neither would be lonesome. They married, and for a long time they lived together and were happy.

Then one afternoon the man came home from hunting and found that the woman had not yet begun to prepare their meal. Instead she was out picking flowers.

The man grew angry.

"I am hungry," he said in a cold voice. "Do you expect me to eat flowers?"

Now the wife, too, became angry. She had picked those flowers to share their beauty with her husband.

"Your words hurt me," she said. "I will live with you no longer."

She turned to the west and began to walk toward the Sun. Her husband followed, but her steps were too quick. He could not catch her. He called her name, but she could not hear him. He went as fast as he could go, but his wife was much faster.

The Sun watched as the husband followed her. The Sun saw how sorry the man was and took pity on him.

"Are you still angry with your wife?" asked the Sun.

"No," said the man, "I was foolish to speak angry words. But I cannot catch her to tell her I am sorry."

"Then I will help you," said the Sun.

The Sun shone its light down on the Earth, in front of the woman. Where its light shone, raspberries grew up. The berries were ripe and looked good to eat, but the woman paid no attention to them and continued walking.

The Sun tried again. It shone down and blueberries grew. They glistened brightly in the sunlight, but the woman paid no attention to them. She only walked on toward the west, leaving her husband farther behind.

Now the Sun tried a third time. Where its beams touched the Earth, blackberries grew up. They were dark and plump, but the woman's anger was too great and she did not see them.

At last the Sun tried its hardest. It shone its light down in the grass right in front of the woman's feet, and strawberries appeared. They glowed like fire in the grass, and the woman had to stop when she saw them in front of her.

She knelt down and plucked one and bit into it. She had never tasted anything like it before. Its sweetness reminded her of how happy she and her husband had been together before they quarreled.

"I must gather some of this fruit for my husband," she said, and she began to pick the berries.

She was still picking them when the man caught up
to her.

"Forgive me for my hard words," he said to her.
And she answered him by sharing the sweetness
of the strawberries.

So it was that strawberries came into the world.

To this day, when the Cherokee people eat strawberries, they are reminded to always be kind to each other; to remember that friendship and respect are as sweet as the taste of ripe, red berries.